Finished
A Fictional Story With Heavenly Truth

Written by: Chuck Kralik

Illustrated by: Terri Melia Hamlin

Copyright 2020

All rights reserved.

There once was a man named Joseph, who lived many years ago.

Joseph was a good man, a humble man. He loved God, and he loved his family. He did what he could to take care of them.

Joseph was a carpenter. He was very good at his craft. Joseph made tables, chairs, benches, and desks.

Joseph was paid for his work, mostly with money.

One time, however, he was paid with a goat and two chickens!

How do you think Joseph's wife, Mary, felt having a goat and two chickens in her house?

Joseph had a son named Jesus. Jesus loved God. Jesus also loved his family.

Even though Jesus was very young, he liked to help Joseph with his many projects.

One day Joseph decided to build a pen to protect his goat and chickens from danger.

Besides, Mary no longer wanted the animals in her house!

While Joseph was constructing the pen for the animals, he observed Jesus a few feet away building something also.

In the dust were two boards that Jesus had crossed over one another.

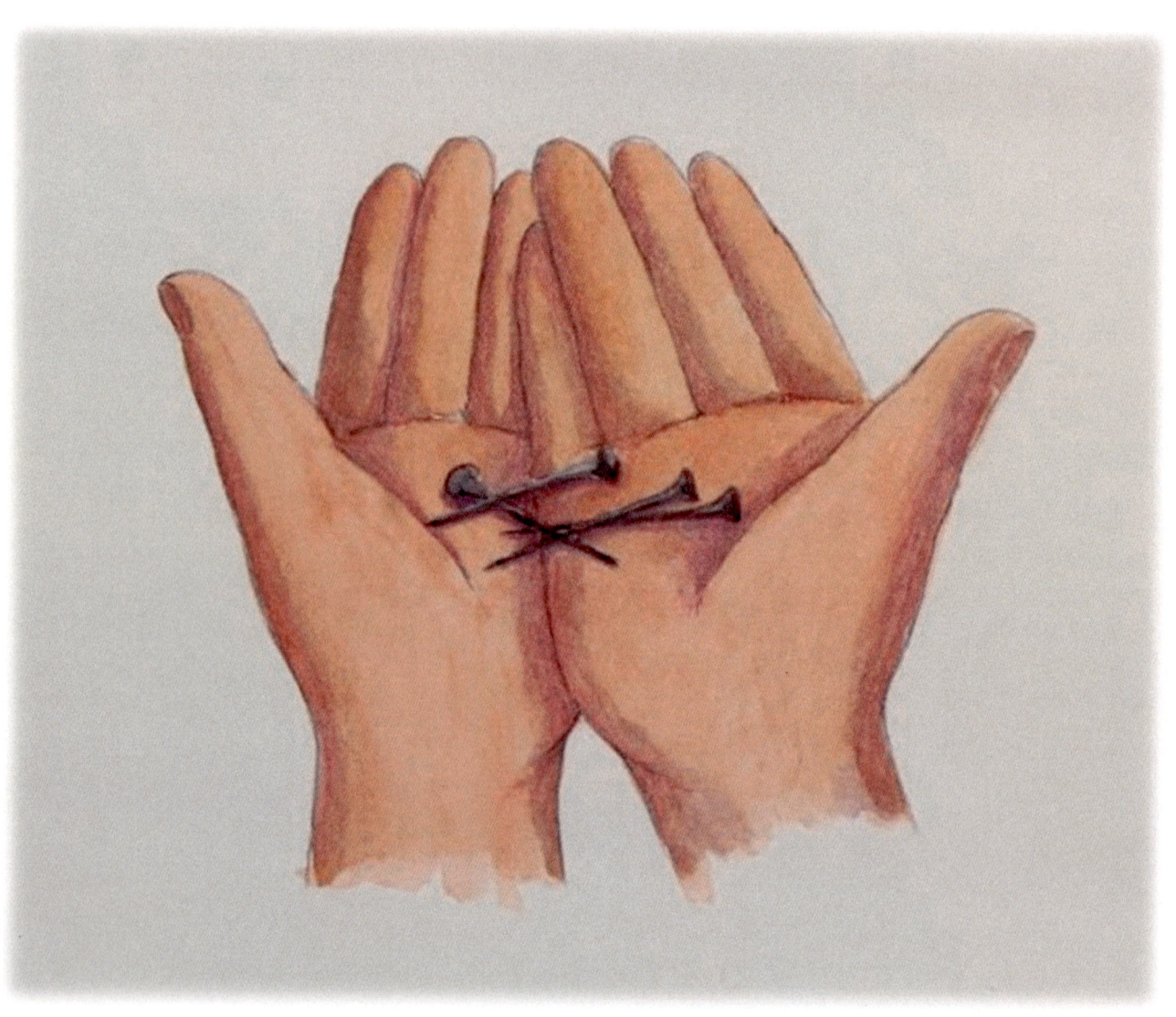

In his hands, Jesus had a few small nails.

Jesus was too little to lift the hammer, so Joseph drove the nails for him.

When the nails were all in place, Joseph asked Jesus, "Now, what do you have to say for yourself?"

Jesus smiled proudly and confidently stated, "It is finished."

"But how will these two boards keep anything safe?" Joseph asked jokingly.
"These two boards will keep us all safe," Jesus answered.

Later that night, Joseph thought about Jesus' words from earlier in the day. "It is finished," he said to himself. "I wonder what Jesus meant by that."

But it was too late to ask Jesus, as he was already asleep.

Appendix

Challenge Questions for Kids:

1. What were the names of the people in the story?

2. Why do you think Mary didn't want the goat and chickens in her house?

3. What did Joseph build for the animals?

4. What did Jesus build with just two boards?

Activities for Kids:

What do you think Joseph's animal pen looked like? Draw a picture of the pen. Don't forget the animals!

What do you think the two boards that Jesus put together looked like? Draw a picture. Do you remember what Jesus said about what he had made?

Bible Truths for Everyone

1. Jesus was a person.

"The Word became flesh and made his dwelling among us. We have seen his glory, the glory of the one and only Son, who came from the Father, full of grace and truth (John 1:14, NIV).

2. Jesus lived a perfect life.

"(Jesus was) tempted in every way, just as we are—yet he did not sin" (Hebrews 4:15, NIV).

3. The cross of Jesus saves people.

" 'For God so loved the world that he gave his one and only Son, that whoever believes in him shall not perish but have eternal life' " (John 3:16, NIV).

Made in the USA
Middletown, DE
21 October 2020